BACK SCHOOL BIGFOOT

By Samantha Berger and Marth

TO WITH OOT

Brockenbrough · Illustrated by Dave Pressler

Arthur A. Levine Books · An Imprint of Scholastic Inc.

For Lin Oliver & Steve Mooser, SCBWI LEGENDS. — SB & MB

For the two art teachers in my life, my dad and
David Runnion from Deer Creek Jr. High. — DP

All rights reserved. Published by Arthur A. Levine Books, an imprint of
Scholastic Inc., Publishers since 1920. SCHOLASTIC and the LANTERN LOGO are
trademarks and/or registered trademarks of Scholastic Inc.

The publisher does not have any control over and does not assume any
responsibility for author or third-party websites or their content.

This book is a work of fiction.
Names, characters, places, and
incidents are either the product of
the author's imagination or are used
fictitiously, and any resemblance to
actual persons, living or dead, business
establishments, events, or locales is entirely
coincidental.

Library of Congress catalog card number: 2016010025

ISBN 978-0-545-85973-8

10 9 8 7 6 5 4 3 2 1   17 18 19 20 21

Printed in China 38

First edition, July 2017

Book design by Charles Kreloff and Steve Ponzo

The artwork for the planning stages and final color art
was created on a Wacom Cintiq using Adobe Photoshop
CC 2017. Finished line art was drawn exclusively with
Staedtler Mars Lumograph 3B Pencils on Strathmore Bristol Paper.

If you think YOU'VE got BIG back-to-school problems, let me tell you, mine are BIGGER!

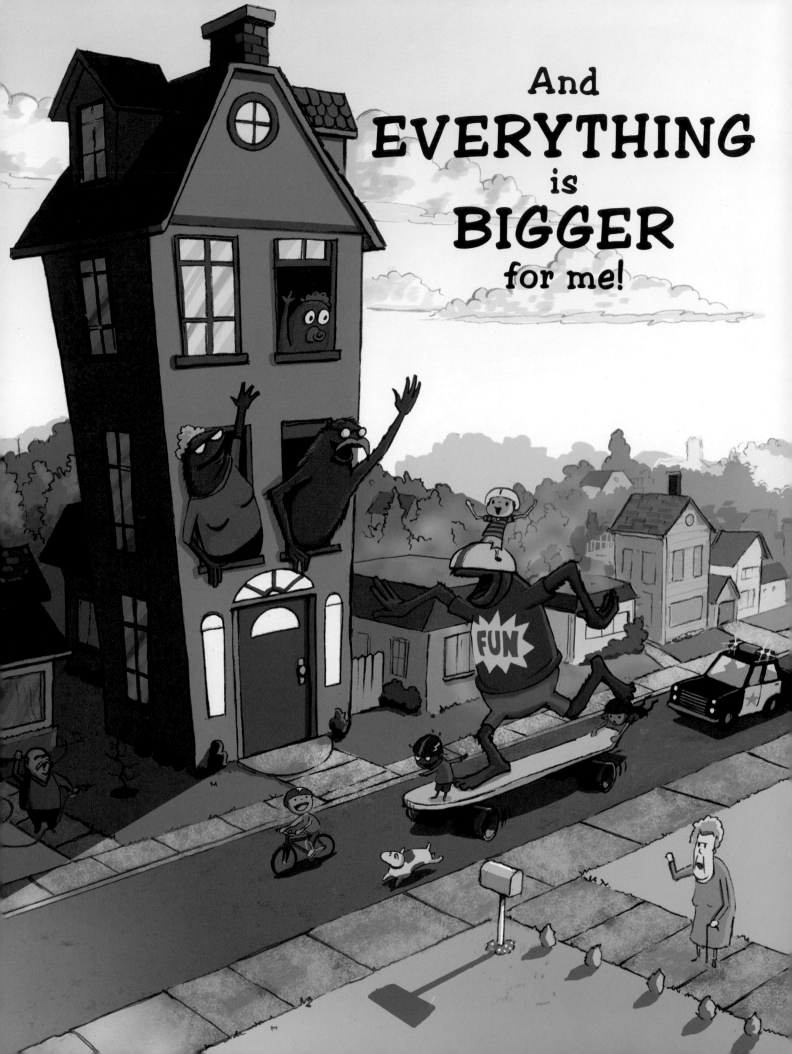

Back-to-school shopping is an **EXTRA-LARGE** job!

Unfortunately, I am EXTRA-EXTRA-LARGE.

A back-to-school haircut takes **ALL DAY,**

because I am
ALL HAIR!

And back-to-school SHOES?

Well, how do you think I got the name **BIGFOOT** in the first place?!

My worries are **BIGGER** than that, though.

What if the bus driver doesn't SEE me when she comes to pick us up?

It could **TOTALLY** happen!

What if I can't stand still
for class pictures?
AGAIN!

What if at lunch . . .
I make a mistake?

The **BIGGEST** mistake in the history of big mistake making?

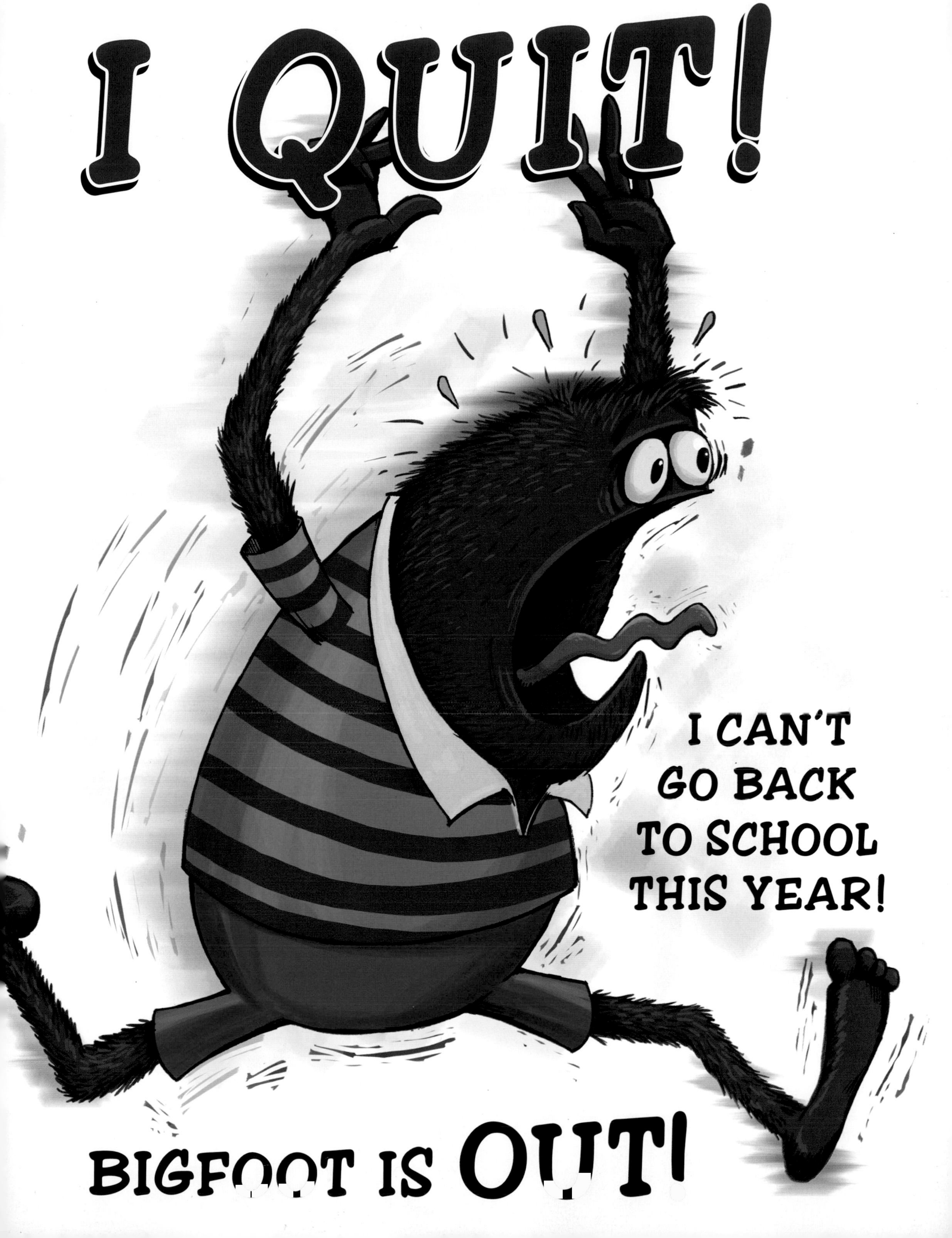
I QUIT!
I CAN'T GO BACK TO SCHOOL THIS YEAR!
BIGFOOT IS OUT!

Even if Miss Sierra Nevada is the
best teacher in our school.

Even if this is the year we get to
study mythological creatures.

Even if I won't get to see all
of my friends again.

Gulp... my friends.

We could do some ENORMOUS
art projects this year . . .

We might go on some
HUMONGOUS field trips . . .

And we will have a
TREMENDOUS
graduation ceremony at the end.

Everyone I love
will be there.

Okay, maybe . . .

Probably . . .

Most likely . . .

AWESOME
NEW HAIRCUT

COOL SUNGLASSES

FAVORITE
T-SHIRT

GLEEP
GORP!

COMFORTABLE
UNDERWEAR

LUCKY ACTION
FIGURE IN POCKET

BACKPACK
MOSTLY
LUNCH

AMAZING NEW
SHOES

I will go back to school this year.

It's a **BIG** step, even for Bigfoot...